Dear Dragon Developing Readers

At the Farm with Dear Dragon

by Marla Conn
Illustrated by Jack Pullan

NORWOODHOUSE PRESS

NOTE TO CAREGIVERS: It is a pleasure to have the opportunity to adapt Margaret Hillert's **Dear Dragon** books for emergent readers! Children will grow and learn to read independently with the boy and his loveable pet dragon as they have done for over 30 years!

The new **Dear Dragon Developing Readers** series gives young children experiences with book concepts and print, and enables them to learn how language works; phonological awareness, letter formation, spaces, words, directionality and oral and written communication.

Emergent Readers are just beginning to control early reading behaviors and require books that have a high level of support including:

- Predictable & repeated language patterns
- Simple story lines
- Familiar topics & vocabulary
- Repetitive words and phrases
- Easy high frequency and decodable words
- Illustrations that support the text

We look forward to watching the lightbulb go on as emerging readers expand their literacy powers; building important strategies for maintaining fluency, correcting error, problem solving new words, and reading and writing for comprehension. The **Dear Dragon Developing Readers** will ultimately guide children through the more complex text in **Dear Dragon Beginning-to-Read Books** as they become curious, confident, independent learners.

Happy Reading!

Marla Con

Marla Conn, MS Ed.
Literacy Consultant/Author

Norwood House Press
Chicago, Illinois

For more information about Norwood House Press please visit our website at: www.norwoodhousepress.com or call 866-565-2900.

Beginning-to-Read™ is a registered trademark of Norwood House Press.

LIBRARY OF CONGRESS CATALOGING-IN-PUBLICATION DATA
Names: Conn, Marla, author. | Pullan, Jack, illustrator.
Title: At the farm with Dear Dragon / by Marla Conn ; illustrated by Jack Pullan.
Description: Chicago, Illinois : Norwood House Press, [2019] | Series: Dear Dragon developing readers | Includes note to caregivers and activities.
Identifiers: LCCN 2018054553 | ISBN 9781684509980 (library edition : alk. paper) | ISBN 9781684043323 (ebook)
Subjects: LCSH: Readers (Primary) | Dragons—Juvenile fiction. | Farm life—Juvenile fiction.
Classification: LCC PE1119 .C6358 2019 | DDC 428.6/2—dc23
LC record available at https://lccn.loc.gov/2018054553

Hardcover ISBN: 978-1-68450-998-0   Paperback ISBN: 978-1-68404-307-1
319N—072019

Manufactured in the United States of America in North Mankato, Minnesota.

WORDS IN THIS BOOK

PICTURE GLOSSARY:

 dog

 cat

 goat

 pig

 hen

 bunny

 horse

 Dear Dragon

 cow

COMMON SIGHT WORDS:

- at
- farm
- is
- the

Dog is at the farm.

Goat is at the farm.

Hen is at the farm.

Horse is at the farm.

Cow is at the farm.

13

Cat is at the farm.

Pig is at the farm.

Bunny is at the farm.

Dear Dragon is at the farm.

Word Work

Using Word Families

1. Name the animals Dear Dragon sees at the farm. Write the animals on a separate sheet of paper.

2. Say the beginning sounds.

   H _____   C _____   G _____
   Fr _____   D _____   P _____
   Ch _____   C _____

3. Say each word family. Use the beginning sounds from above to make new words:

   uck   oat   ick
   en   ig   ow
   og   at

4. How many animal names did you make? How many new words did you discover?

Activity

On a separate sheet of paper, draw a picture of what your farm would look like, using inspiration from the image below. Write a sentence about the animals that can be found at your farm.

About the Author

Marla Conn has been an educator and literacy specialist for over 30 years. Witnessing the amazing moment when the "lightbulb goes on" as young children process print and learn how to read independently inspired a passion for creating books that support aspiring readers. She has a strong belief that all children love stories and have a natural curiosity for books. Marla enjoys reading, writing, playing with her 2 golden doodles and spending time with family and friends.

About the Illustrator

A talented and creative illustrator, Jack Pullan is a graduate of William Jewell College. He has also studied informally at Oxford University and the Kansas City Art Institute. He was mentored by the renowned watercolor artists, Jim Hamil and Bill Amend. Jack's work has graced the pages of many enjoyable children's books, various educational materials, cartoon strips, as well as many greeting cards. Jack currently resides in Kansas.